NIGHT GAMES

SUE MYDLIAK

I dedicate this book to my fans, for without them I would not be where I am today.

ACKNOWLEDGMENTS

I'd like to express my gratitude for my husband's patience while I wrote this and for putting up with a messy house.

---

*P*eople call me weird, hood wicked and crazy. I say, their self-esteem sucks. I get it though. Does it bother me? Hell no. What goes around comes around I always say . . . and I come right back around. Fools. They never see it coming.

I'm not what you would call your typical American male. Not even close. I'm moody, a loner, don't like crowds, and I'm irritable when hungry. *You* do not want to be around me when that happens. That's just half of what I am, the other half is bizarre, freaky and dark.

My name is Jon, Jonathan Harker. I'm 22 years old and that's where I've stayed for the past . . . oh, say . . . 300 years? I've stopped counting. I found no purpose in it.

I will say I am good-looking. At least I think I am. I've got dark hair, dark eyes, and pale skin. I'm muscular without looking like I've taken steroids. My other attributes are I'm fast. I can outrun a train. I also heal quickly and I'm hard to kill.

My clothing, well, I like black. Black jeans, black dress

shirts, and black shoes. Color doesn't look good against my skin. Makes me look . . . dead and I have an impeccable, yet, expensive taste. You won't see me at some mall. Have you seen them? I believe their buyers have no sense of taste.

I have a tailor come. He knows my body and how I like my clothes to fit and he'll only get the best material money can buy. *He* has good *taste*. Where did I find him? I have friends with the same tastes as myself. They told me about him, in fact, they were eager for me to *try him out*. So, I did and they were right! Friends, can't live without them.

I go to college. My degree? I haven't figured that one out yet. I tried to be a welder, but the bright light from the welding torch burned my skin. Nothing else didn't appeal to me, so I just take anything that looks interesting. Seems pointless I know, but it does have its benefits. For one, I'm on the hockey team. Seems I'm good at it, especially with speed. They say I could be the next Patrick Kane.

One day, a cloudy day, a *perfect* day, I went down to the cafeteria for a . . . bite. She was drop-dead gorgeous and she had a figure that would make any man's heart stop. Mine, of course, was already, but that's beside the point.

Her name was Vanessa, Vanessa Cleary. I saw her at the far end, next to the windows. She was with two other girls who weren't bad looking, but she out shone them both. I've heard stuff about her, stuff from my coven. She wasn't to be trusted, in fact, she ate guys like me for breakfast. Was she a problem? Yes and no. No one from my coven is missing, not yet, but I'll keep my eye on this one. This information gave me all I needed to know . . . for now, besides, I like a female who is troublesome. Sometimes it's the bad ones that I find most favorable. She needed to be stopped though and killing her wouldn't be an option, it would be my last resort if necessary.

I positioned myself in her line of vision and watched.

I entered her mind. Fascinating, but wow, a lot of static. Usually, a human's mind is busy, especially women's. I don't know how they manage to not go crazy. Men are simpler. We have only one thing is on our minds. Anything else is just . . . meh.

I got her attention right away. She felt me. Knew I was watching. She smiled.

I gave her a smile back. Nothing big. Just a sensual kind, where just one side of my mouth goes up a bit and my eyes called her in.

She stood up. Walked toward me and said, "I don't know why I'm here, but I'm sure you do."

"By all means." And I gestured to the chair across from me.

"Alright."

"So, Vanessa what brings you here today?"

Her eyes were blue. I like that in a girl.

She paused. Then replied, "I don't know exactly, but I have class. You'll have to excuse me, I'm a bit flustered at the moment."

"Aren't we all?" I was smooth.

Again, another strange look.

"I'm hungry."

"I'm *hungry* too." I gave her another of my winning smiles.

"I see."

My hand touched hers. She flinched. I looked deep into her eyes. Our connection — strong and she sensed it.

"I'd like to eat too, but not here. Not now. How about you meet me by the J building. Let's say around 6:00 p.m. Will you?" I took her hand in mine this time.

"Alright . . . 6 it is. See you."

"Yes. See you." I let her go.

Her friends, while in their excitability bombarded her with questions. *What did he want? Did he ask you any questions?*

3

If so, what? Oh, he so cute, so handsome! Do you know him? Do you have a class with him? All the while they looked at me. I kept my cool. Lounged back in my chair. One leg extended out, while the other was bent at the knee. I had this debonair look about me. Yeah, I'm a ladies man.

---

*a*fter I watched her and her friends walk away, I got up, adjusted myself and went home.

I had a game tonight. We were playing against a team called the Goonies or Goons. They were thugs. Played dirty and got away with a lot of shit. I've kept my cool when we had played them before. Didn't want who I was to come out, but not tonight. Tonight I will show them who the *goon* is.

I usually get to the ice rink an hour or so early. I don't like rushing. Warm-ups are essential to my playing. It also gets my mind to focus on what I need to do. We would win tonight.

I sometimes played goalie, but not tonight, tonight I was a defenseman, right defense. This was my favorite position. It was up to me and the other defensemen to keep the incoming play out of our zone. We block shots, break up passes, and that's where I excelled. There will be blood on the ice tonight.

But before any of that can happen, I needed to get home. I packed my gear into the car. I needed to hunt. I needed all my strength for the game.

Now my home is a modest home. Nothing fancy. I bought it in an area that most people wouldn't come around. Seems that in any town you go into, the older side is not always the best. That suits me to a 'T'.

The area is gang infested, but that didn't scare me. I believe that *they* are more scared of *me*. Anyway, my house is old, Victorian to be exact. Gray in color. An old wrought-iron fence, still sturdy after all these years, protected my property.

I had bought this house when I was changed.

One night, on my way to my car, something or someone knocked me down. Hard. Surprised and a bit pissed off, I got to my knees when, again, something knocked me back down.

"If I were you I'd stop moving. It'll only make things worse for you."

The voice was deep. The hairs on the back of my neck stood up.

"Who, who are you? What do you want?"

"You."

I didn't know what he met by *you*, but I decided to give him my wallet. I wouldn't fight.

"You can have my wallet! I don't care! Just don't hurt me!"

He laughed, "I don't want *your wallet*. I want *you*."

Before my next breath, he yanked my head to the side and bit down. Pain shot down my neck and I remembered, as I lay there the ground, and the pebbles . . . the cars in the lot . . . they grew dim. My body wasn't my own anymore. I couldn't feel anything. Numbness took over and in the distance, I thought I heard . . . maybe it was me . . . I don't . . .

When I woke, my throat burned. I panicked. I didn't know what had happened to me or why I felt this way, but it needed to stop. I had to stop it.

Wobbling on my feet, I must have looked drunk. People just looked at me like I was possessed. I felt like it.

Loud noises bombarded me. Cars, brakes, talking, laughing, insects, even my own footsteps! The loudness of it all!

"I can't bear it! Make it stop!"

Then, a woman, I'll never forget her. She came up to me and asked if I was alright. I turned my head. My eyes drank her in. Captured her. She was mine. I heard her heart. Her blood coursing through her veins and it excited me. My throat burned worse. Just the very thought of blood made it burn deeper, harder.

I grabbed her and before she could make a noise, she was dead. The burning stopped, but just for a moment. It came back again. Worse.

*T*hat's how it all started. Of course, it's been many years since that night and I've gotten quite used to it. In fact, I indulge myself almost every night! I'm not proud of myself, but hey, a man's got to do, what a man's got to do and I do it very well.

Anyway, as soon as I got home, I dashed into the nearest wooded area . . . Pilcher Park. Great place for picnics I hear, but I don't do picnic's, mine is sort of . . . fast food if you know what I mean. Just grab and go!

There were a few people there, some with family, couples, and some just out by themselves. Those are the ones to go after. Then, there are those who go for walks. A possibility there. One being good, but when there are two, I can have dessert! Sounded tempting.

They were young. I'd say in their mid-twenties. Totally into themselves and not aware that someone, me, was watching them. I like to play with my food, makes it more appealing. I didn't play this time. I had places to go and time was of the essence.

With muscles tensed. I felt myself bulk up. It's hard to

explain. Imagine bubbles as you blow from a pipe. Blow hard and they start to cluster. Growing bigger and bigger. Bad analogy, but it's the only thing I could come up with. Doesn't hurt, not now. It did in my earlier years. I hated it but having that reaction to it, aided in the killing process. It pissed me off, the pain. So much so, that I'd take that anger out on my victim.

The other changes that take place . . . my fangs. My lips curl back to give way when they descend. They're big, pointy and can chew leather up like it was butter. Nice right? I've been known to admire them.

Another attribute in my transition are my eyes. They get red, a cold, and steely red. I'm a sight let me tell you. I don't know what's scarier to my victim, my eyes or my brute strength. I would have to say both.

They're doomed right from the get go. My delight . . . watching the fear, but I have two to deal with, so I have to be extremely quick. The less noise the better. Don't want to bring any attention to the site. Not until I'm gone.

I got the male out of the way first. Males can be over-protective of their mate. Understandably. Females, as you might guess, are easy. I don't like to see them squirm, so I compel them. Then, it's all downhill from there. They were an excellent choice. Young blood always is.

I arrived at the rink an hour early. I felt strong, determined. My muscles still tense, but not enough to put me into vampiric mode. Takes a while to retain my natural good looks, though being in my full vampire mode, I'm quite the catch.

The other guys on my team, we get along. I think they may know something, but I don't see how. I never let on about my true nature. Tonight though . . . they may never want me to play on their team again.

I smiled.

Warm-up time ended. I was first to play. I was ready for them. I was the enforcer of our team. My job was to protect my teammates and make the opponents think twice about making any cheap shots at them. Enforcers also are never afraid to pick a fight. They got that right.

The game was going well. Everyone played fair, until we got ahead of them, 6 to 3. They weren't happy. That's when they decided to play dirty.

Number 44, Chris, our team, had the puck. He was our hat trick and the best by far.

He had just crossed the blue line when number 14 of the other team came and tripped him. The refs didn't see it, though I don't see how they couldn't! That's ok, I can fix that. I'll play *ref* my way.

Before he could turn around with the puck, I, in a flash, brought him down . . . hard. He was out. No one saw who done it. By the time I had done this, I was back to my original spot. To others, it looked as though he fainted. A bad faint, for his nose, was broken. I believe he was their hat trick. Too bad.

By the time the game had ended we had won 9 to 3. The other team had four injured, bloodied men. No one could explain how though. They chucked it up to really bad skating or bad ice. Either way, they didn't suspect me.

Nevertheless, I had to get ready to meet up with Vanessa. As soon as I got home, I hopped into the shower, shaved, then chose my outfit with care. Black pants, shirt, and shoes. Doesn't get any better than that. I studied myself in the mirror.

"Who could resist?"

I got there in record time, as usual.

I found a spot, just inside the doors. It was busy as usual. Night classes had already started and I didn't look too much out of the ordinary, though I did get some looks from other girls. Yeah, I let them feast their eyes on me. Why not? I've got the looks. I do love the ladies.

"Hi, Jon!"

She looked great! She was into black herself. Black boots, leggings, little skirt with a tight top and jacket. Yeah, I could see possibilities here, but then again, there seemed to be something about her that I connected to. I couldn't explain it.

"You're on time. I like that. Why don't you and I go for a walk? I know a great place. Out of the way. We can have some privacy."

"Sure, whatever you want."

Whatever I want huh? I like her already and I haven't done my magic yet.

"I'm glad you're so willing."

I took her hand in mine and we walked down by the river, up a ways from the building.

The dead leaves crunched beneath our feet and the smell . . . earthy. As we continued on our path, which was laden with twigs and rustling foliage, a different feeling came about. I couldn't pin point it, but she definitely was something else. Not human.

I found two boulders to sit on. It was a perfect spot. Well hidden, away from prying eyes. She sat close and the sound of her heart beat loud and clear. Music.

"You look nice tonight and you smell delici . . . wonderful." Almost killed it.

"I'm not wearing any perfume."

"Oh, then it must be your shampoo. Is that honey and jasmine?"

She took a lock of her hair, sniffed and said, "No, it's T Gel."

"Oh! *Smells nice.*"

"Really? I always thought it smelled medicinal." And sniffed again.

Seeing how I was scoring out on conversation I made my first move. Inching my way closer, I took all of her essences in. This was going to be some night.

"Can you stop sniffing me? You're freaking me out, not to mention I'm uncomfortable. What are you? Part dog?"

"I'm sorry. It's just that you're so irresistible. I can't get enough of you. Would you mind if I kissed you?"

"I guess not."

Not the response I had hoped for. In fact, she didn't seem all that excited, but I'm not one to complain.

She leaned in and when our lips touched I got a peculiar feeling. She . . . I didn't get that *wow* factor I normally do. Instead, something told me I got myself into a mess.

I leaned back. Studied her hard. I couldn't figure her out. I was right, she wasn't human, I mean, she was, but she was something else.

"This is such a giveaway isn't it?" As she pointed at her lips, "For being one of them, you're not very smooth. At least those like you could tell right away. You're quite old and yet, you're trying to act as if you were born in this century. I hate to burst your bubble, but you're failing miserably."

She stood up.

"I should have changed right as you kissed me. Would have been funny to have seen your face! But my mother told me to never do anything drastic on a first date. Guys like you are pathetic leeches."

"Leech?" I hated that name. I'm not a leech, nor have I ever been.

"Look, I've got to go. I should have said no to you all along, but I couldn't resist. Besides, I don't date vampires, I kill them, but in your case . . . meh, not worth the time, nor the effort."

She started to walk back when she stopped.

"Oh, and don't bother with my friends. They're like me as well."

Then proceeded back toward the J building.

What just happened?

---

*V*anessa, she's a bad ass, kills vampires for fun. I being the *enforcer*, both on the ice and in my Coven, it is my job to make sure my Coven isn't being attacked or messed around with.

I don't make the rules. I obey the Grand Sire of our Coven only, the Domencio Coven. It was he, who made me what I am today. To disobey is death.

I hated him. For a long time in fact. I hated myself. I'm sure all newborns feel that way, but they got over it. I did, eventually. Took a long time to see reason. I think he sensed that in me as well. He more or less left me to my own devices, which I now understood why. I respected him and that's how I got to be where I am today.

Last year, our Coven was under attack. We didn't know by who or by what, but within a week seven of our members were dead.

No, we didn't find their bodies. Vampires are usually burned, as to keep us from coming back. The way we found out came to us in boxes. Inside were their rings. You see,

Lord Domencio gave us rings as a sign, our loyalty to our Coven. Shows us and others who we belong to.

Domencio had asked for my presence and so I came before him, bowed of course.

"My Lord, what do you wish?"

"Rise. As you well know, we have lost seven members. I want this thing, person, whatever it is brought to me."

Now, Domencio is fearsome. His greatness should never be taken lightly. Many fools have lost their lives.

The first time I saw him I couldn't speak. He scared the shit out of me. There I was, newly changed and there he sat, on a granite throne, ornate with gargoyles on either side. He was lanky, broad shouldered and his overall presence . . . gaunt. His hands were boney, with nails, sharp and long. He wore a burgundy robe and shoes.

"Yes, my Lord."

As I turned to leave, he stopped me.

"Your life depends on this. Do not fail me."

Usually, I'm very confident in my abilities to get what I want, but with that last word hung over my head, I had some reservations.

Vanessa wasn't easy either and being a shape shifter, she could be anything! My plan, go back to the college and watch her. See who she hangs around with and follow them. Maybe with my good looks and charm, I could persuade or compel them to tell me about her. Oh, one more thing, I had something on her. Something that not even she knew, or did she? My Coven isn't aware of it, which makes this order hard for me. It would, no, it *is* life changing. Just hope that lady luck would be on my side.

*A*s Vanessa, sat there, ignoring her friends, that connection I had felt, lingered. It hadn't been annoying and would go away when we were apart, but anytime she was near — there it was! I kept my eyes on her. Watched how she reacted with her friends. A hint of a smile would appear, even a laugh, but for the most part, she just listened. By the looks of things, I would say she found them funny and perhaps a dumb.

I entered her mind. I normally don't, but I needed to know what made her tick. What were her thoughts? My conclusions were correct, she did feel that way about them. So why hang out with them then? Women, confusing as all hell, but man cannot live without them.

"Emily, honestly, don't you know anything? Shakespeare is the world's best-known writer of them all. His stories and plays will live forever. If you don't understand them, why take the class?"

"I needed the credit!" Emily. She had a Pixie cut hair style. She reminded me of an elf. A cute one at that. Red lips and cheeks that I'm sure her grandmother must have pinched when she was a baby. Not very bright though. Poor girl.

"I don't know about you, but tonight is a full moon and you know what that means! *Party time* at the Blood Moon." Vanessa said.

"Oh, I can't wait, I've been itching to get my hands on some hunky shifters. They must be itching too." Emily squealed.

"Now, remember, if we want to see some action, we must apply ourselves accordingly. Which means Emily, no more skirts. You look like a schoolmarm," Vanessa spoke sharply.

"I do not. Besides, I thought that wearing a skirt, commando style would make things a whole lot easier."

The stern look on Vanessa's face told her all she needed to know.

"Oh, alright then, the leather treatment it is," Emily sighed.

"Also, if I'm getting busy, keep away. I don't like threesomes. The man is mine and mine alone."

"Vanessa, what if the cops come in like they did last time. It wasn't a pretty sight and you know they've been keeping tabs on the place. I've heard a lot of other shifters are going over to Morpheus. Maybe we should try going over there."

Now, that one showed promise. I wonder what her name is.

She was different. In that, I mean, she didn't come across as dumb, not like Emily. No, she had that refine look about her. Class. Intelligent. I'd say she came second to Vanessa.

I liked her. Not sure if she's . . . no, she's a shifter alright. From what I've observed of this group, shifter women are tough, they get what they want when they want it, and they don't share. Though I wouldn't mind sharing. Mother always did say it was the polite thing to do.

"Kate, I'm not going to Morpheus that place stinks.

Besides, all the good wolves are here. Over there you don't know what you're getting. It's too risky. No, we'll be alright, just keep alert and if anyone one of us sees something out of place let me know. Deal?"

"Deal!"

"Ah, Kate. That's her name. Ok, Kate, hope to meet you tonight."

Now to figure out where this Blood Moon was? Never heard of the place, but it sounded like a bar that only shifters go to. Well, I'll just have to crash that place. See what's so special about it?

---

6

*A*t home, I looked up Blood Moon and found it to be on the East side. An ok neighborhood. Weird things have happened in that area. Cult like things. I remembered reading where a ritual had taken place and at the sight, they found what is called an Athame, a ritual knife. It is used to cast a magic circle, called the quarters or elements. They usually use this for weddings or an initiation. This time it was used in a killing.

Should be an interesting night. I'll go and see what all the hoopla is about and see my girl Vanessa in action.

The day rolled by slow. I'm what you would call impatient. Things have to happen right away, fast. Not like this.

I paced back and forth. Looked at the clock. Five minutes had gone by. Five, fucking minutes! That's it.

I went off to hunt or something to expel this pent up energy. If anything it'll make the time go by faster. Maybe I'll just play around. My way of not killing anyone, but tapping them. You know, a sip here and there. Sometimes, tapping leads to other things, which I'm always game. Though if you know anything about vampires, having someone drink from you is very erotic.

The night held promises or so I hoped. I drove over to the East side first, just to check it out. I was right, the area wasn't too bad. A bit seedy. A whore here and there. The usual night life.

I turned the corner when I found the bar, nothing came close to what I thought it would look like. Talk about dramatic. The outside was painted black, with stars traveling all over it. It was the night sky and above it a huge, glowing moon.

"How in the hell did I manage to not see this?"

It was quite the building. One has to wonder what the inside must look like. Even during the day, it looked ominous.

The sun finally went down. I couldn't wait to see what this place looked like from the inside. I could only imagine and with that being said the excitement grew. I dressed in my black attire, slicked back my hair and cologne. I had to drench myself in it. We vampires, so I'm told, have a certain scent. Shifters and Weres are sensitive to it and seeing how this place wasn't for my kind, I needed to hide my scent as much as possible. It'll be dark I'm sure, so I have that on my side.

I drove and parked a bit down the road. I couldn't just enter like everyone else, the bouncer would surely know what I was. Entering via the back door was the key . . . or window, whatever I could find available . . . then I remembered. How could I be so stupid? I rarely use this ability, haven't needed too much, but it would come in very handy this time. I would enter via the front door.

The line was long, but I hadn't planned on standing in it. No, mine would be inconspicuous. Like a fly who zoomed in unnoticed, but later is seen. That's the plan I had in mind. I closed my eyes and made myself feel light as air. Around me, the air stirred. I felt myself thin out till I was nothing but a fine, black vapor. Then, flew into a spot way in the back corner. It was dark, as I had imagined. The bar, at the opposite side of me, was like any other bar, but one thing different, the bartender was a half man, half wolf. Quite the charmer from what I could tell. The ladies poured themselves over him. Nice. I have to say, it wasn't all that impressive inside, but what made it interesting, no, provocative, were the cliental. Scantily dressed women, and beefy men with shirts unbuttoned or none at all danced out on the floor. Not just any dance mind you, this was X rated. Hell, even I had a hard time containing myself.

There I sat, taking it all in. I started to think that we needed a bar like this.

A woman, waitress, came up to my table and asked if I wanted anything.

"Gin and tonic."

She gave me a smile. A long, lingering smile and said, "Anything for you sugar. *Anything* at all."

I didn't reply back. Just smiled.

In the meantime, I didn't see Vanessa yet, I knew she'd be around at some point. In the meantime, I'll just watch and try to control myself.

I took notice this time on the décor. Being dark it was hard to see anything. The only lights that were on were above the dance floor and the bar. The rest of the place in total darkness. I understood why too. People were getting busy in the booths, at tables, hell, they were getting busy out on the dance floor.

My waitress came back, only this time she had changed her clothing. This time she had decided for the more *natural* look.

"Here's your drink. Enjoy?" Her hands trailed down her curves, slow and tantalizing.

"Miss . . . "

"Cinnamon." Her voice, sultry and oh, so appealing.

"Cinnamon, tell me something do you always work . . . well, in the buff?" The temperature seemed to have gotten hotter all of a sudden, though we vampires don't feel the differentiating of degrees usually.

"Well, I'll let you in on a little secret . . ." She made herself comfortable next to me in the booth, "I only do this when I see someone I really want and I want you."

"Really now? I'm liking what I see as well. Very much."

"So, what are you waiting for? An invitation? I'm here for the taking." And with that, she started in on me. First, she kissed my lips, then went down my neck. There she lingered as her tongue did things I never knew was possible . . . then a thought crossed my mind.

I grabbed her by her waist and lifted her off me.

"As much as I would love this to continue, I can't. I'm . . . expecting a lady, um, wolf . . . I'm expecting a female companion tonight and she should be here any moment."

"Oh, that's too bad. I had plans for you. Big plans." Her fingers walked up my chest to my lips.

"I'm sure you did, but maybe some other time?"

"Here's my number, call me."

She had written her number down on my palm. Where she had gotten the pen from I have no idea. Didn't want to know, but I would give her a call. Definitely.

After she left I got back to searching for Vanessa.

"Hello." Another sexy voice out of nowhere spoke.

I looked up and there before me was this creature, a gorgeous creature. She wore black leather pants, tight, and a tank top, white, no bra. It revealed much. I had died again and gone to shifter heaven.

"Hello. Can I help you?" Dumb line, but at that moment that's all I could come with. Steady man, steady.

She sat down, next to me. Put her right arm around the back of my neck and while the other started to unbutton my shirt. The women here don't mess around.

"Oh, you can help me in so many ways. In fact, you can start right now . . . I'm not shy."

"I can see that. You're a wiz at buttons." I grabbed her hand. If I hadn't, she'd probably have my pants undone. Don't get me wrong, I like women, but I have standards, this wasn't one of them. "Let's take things a bit slow, shall we. We have all night, why rush into it?"

"I hate conversations. I like results. Your result I like very much." For a woman, shifter, she was extremely strong. Not a problem for me though.

I realized that I was going to have problems. The women here are hot to trot. My turn to get the ball rolling.

"Tell me something, do you know a Vanessa Cleary?" I asked. Apparently, it turned her on. Next thing I knew I was laid out on the booth seat, with her on top.

"First, we kiss, then answers, no?"

I didn't notice before, but she had a slight accent. What I did notice was she was horny as all get out. In fact, all the women here were.

"Alright . . . but that's all," her hands started exploring, I grabbed them, "Kissing only."

It was light at first, lips barely touching, then deeper. My muscles began to ripple as we delved deeper into the art of it

At some point, soon, I had to stop or the true me would soon be known. She . . . was a pro.

"Ok, ok . . . that was, whoa, unbelievable. Have you always kissed . . . never mind. Vanessa, do you know her?"

"Oh, yes. I know. Now we strip."

7

"*N*o. Let's talk."

She pouted those luscious lips, then gave an impish grin.

"But of course, she is strong and she like a leader. More kissing now."

She went in for the kill, all arms and a sex drive to boot, but I counter attacked with a *face-off*. My eyes connected with hers straight away. She was all mine now.

"Tell me something that you know about Vanessa Cleary."

I could tell she was fighting me, but I had the upper hand on this . . . I'm a vampire, don't mess with me.

"She is a shifter. A wolf." Her voice, low and seductive would allure any poor sap. This chick was good.

"Anything else I should know?"

Still struggling, she gave incriminating evidence against her friend.

"She kills vampires for fun." A deep, guttural laugh burst forth. This chick needed serious help, but not from me.

'Well, thank you . . .'"

"Darya."

"Darya, thank you. When I leave, you will remember nothing, nothing at all. It'll be as if we never met."

I scooted out from the booth and faded in with the darkness. Little did she know I hid myself up in the rafters of the joint.

I needed to find Vanessa and fast. Thanks to Darya I knew her agenda. It now came down to me.

It wasn't long till she made an appearance. Her taste in clothes met with my approval. Her style of fashion were tight jeans, a white tank top, no bra and spiky, black heels. Nice. Her hair, blonde and long came down over her shoulders. Silky. Shiny.

She met up with some other people, friends from college, and other acquaintances. Nothing notable about them, but what I did observe is that they all seemed to have the same body type. In that their sinewy form didn't mean they were weak. On the contrary, that kind doesn't put up with a lot of shit. They headed toward the bar. She bought. The bar keeper, as I said, part wolf and man . . . he was a piece of work. The man part was all brawn. His white shirt, unbuttoned at the top, exposed his massive chest with fur with his sleeves rolled up past his elbows. His arms were nothing but muscle. Tight. I bet his punch packed a bunch. Wouldn't want to piss him off.

From what I saw from the waist up was a threat, I can only imagine the bottom half.

"Damn, the dude has muscles."

I wanted to go down and try my luck with her again, but that would prove disastrous on many levels. There were many of them and only one of me. I'd be fine for five minutes then I'd be an hors d'oeuvre. No, better stay put.

As I watched, she seemed agitated. Her eyes kept searching, searching for what I wondered?

Wolves have a keen sense of smell and good eye sight, but

she's not in wolf form. Maybe that doesn't work until she changed. She sensed something or someone that's for sure. I wonder . . .

After about a half hour had gone by, she and her friends got out on the dance floor. All night the smell of hormones reacting to the beat of the music made for an exciting night. These shape shifters weren't shy at all. They let it all hang out and I mean *all hangout.*

Vanessa wasn't bashful either. She had some muscle bound dude touch her wherever and she became quite turned on, not that she wasn't already. As it were, she reciprocated back. Rather sexy flirtation of the hottest kind I've ever observed.

It had gotten quite intense as Mr. Hunky hip thrust his way toward her back side and much to her delight she hip grinded back. Seemed to be a popular dance.

All during this, my body started to react and not in a good way. My mood changed as well. It came on slow and gradually increased as I continued to watch Vanessa and her partner.

Shaking it off wouldn't do. It would be like shaking off the need for blood . . . not going to happen. I couldn't place it.

Then it hit me. Something I hadn't felt in a long time. Something that I, more or less, forgotten. In my position, there was no need.

Jealousy. I thought about it and the more I did, the more it made perfect sense, as did the connection. Vanessa was my soulmate. I didn't know how that could be. Vampires and werewolves shouldn't be compatible, but the signs are all here.

I had to get out. I'd wait for her outside. If I had stayed any longer a fight would have ensued.

I became a filmy, black nothingness and seeped out through a vent in the ceiling.

"Jon!" Vanessa caught my scent.

The alley just across from Blood Moon would prove an excellent vantage point. I could still see the front of the building.

Within seconds, Vanessa came out. Enraged, her eyes darted toward me, though I was still in the shadows, she knew.

Having difficulties my love? I thought.

8

*S*he charged right for me.

"I know you are here. You can't hide from me. I can smell your filthy, rancid, stench. Show yourself?"

I kept my distance. Hovered just above her, I stayed quiet . . . for a little bit. Just long enough though to feel her out. What her game plan was. Or, I wouldn't say anything at all and annoy the hell out of her. Either way, it wouldn't be pleasant.

I love a woman scorned, makes everything a little spicy. Never a dull moment I grant you but does make for a most difficult night.

"How dare you come to Blood Moon. You have no place, no right to be there. Show yourself."

My, her panties were in a bunch. Too bad I can't offer her request, but I decided to offer a conversation. A *small* conversation.

"I do apologize for not making an appearance, but I'm partial to this type of meeting, especially when, one such as yourself, are prone to lash out irrationally. As for showing up at the Blood Moon, I merely wanted to see what your friends were all excited about. It's not that impressive. In fact, I've seen better places. Granted their clientele behaved more civilize, though I must say, everyone, seemed to enjoy each other immensely at your place."

She grew even angrier. That's good Jon, piss off more why don't you?

"You don't understand our kind and why would you. You're a vampire. A nosy one at that. Did you come to spy on me? Felt defeated? Did your huge ego deflate when I turned you down? You are pathetic. So full of yourself. That's the problem with your kind. All you know how to do is kill. It's all about satisfying your need. Our kind, yeah, we kill, only when necessary, not out of need. We treat our kind with love, honor and with dignity."

I had to laugh, "Dignity? You call dancing the way you did, dignity? It looked more like an orgy!"

One leap. That's all it took. One leap into the air and she changed into a wolf. Unique in the process, took less than a second. Was I impressed? Hell yeah! I've never watched a shifter change.

"Tell me something? How are you going to attack if you can't even see me? Waste of energy."

She ran up the walls and back down again. She knew where I stood, just couldn't attack.

Quite futile if you ask me. I grew tired of her games.

"Before you tire yourself out, I have a question."

She changed back. Naked. Shape Shifters were terribly hard on clothes, but I liked what I saw. Pity I couldn't do something about it.

"What?"

"Have you ever felt anything between us?"

"You mean pure, unadulterated hate? *Yes*. Why?"

"No, that's not what I meant, I mean it is . . . well, from your stand point I can see your reasoning. No, I mean . . . I feel a connection. Like there's a link between you and I. Don't you feel that?"

She looked sick. "You've got to be kidding me right? A shifter and a vampire. Connected? This is too funny! What mojo juice were you drinking at the Blood Moon anyway?"

I knew better than to have asked. I also knew she'd react this way, but I had to put it out there.

I was right next to her. Close enough to touch and I wanted to touch, believe me.

In tones that were quite soft, I said, "It's hard to explain. Next time, when you sense me close by, listen to your body. Being a shifter I thought for sure you'd be more attuned to your body. Listen. It's there. Maybe when you do feel that connection we can talk, until then . . . oh, by the way, stay away from my Coven. Kill one more and you'll see a drastic decline in numbers with yours."

With that, I vanished. Left her stranded, naked and alone.

9

I didn't know much about shape shifters and there had been talk about a line, border if you will, that separates them from us. Where this boundary was, I had no idea.

The Blood Moon last night gave me some idea into their life style. A full moon was out last night. Humans change to Werewolves when that happens. What I didn't know is that it also makes them horny. That needed some investigation.

I went to the library downtown. It being the oldest, built in 1875, I felt that it would be the ideal place to start.

Now, downtown it is old. Like most towns, it has a few restaurants, Baseball Stadium, and a sorted businesses, but it's not like others I've seen. It doesn't have cute little shops and eateries. I think that's why I like it so much here. It has a river that separates the West side from the East side. Its river had been, at one time, a working river, still is to this day, just not as much.

Crossing over one of its many bridges, I turned the corner next to the parking deck. The library was just down the street on the right.

Taking the steps to its doors, I opened them. The smell of books, leather, paper and floor wax hit me. Reminds me of my past.

My father, from what I can remember, had a library. He had shelves, upon shelves, full of books. He could always be found there after dinner. Reading and smoking his pipe. I wasn't allowed in, only when he was present

The stairs to the upper floor were in the middle of the library. I hate stairs, only because in public I can't be myself. I have to do things the *slow* way. People already steer clear of me. I clenched my hands and took to them . . . one, by, one. God.

I walked from aisle to aisle until I found the section and the book, Full Moon. Of course, what else would it be called?

The nearest chair to me stood in a corner, no window. Perfect.

The cover was plain, nothing spectacular about it. This author apparently didn't want his book to sell. I, for one, wouldn't have bought it, the cover didn't stand out.

One of the chapters dealt with the word *full moon* in different languages. Big deal. I moved on further, though I hadn't made any headway.

I set the book down and headed off to the reference desk. An older gentleman, about 50ish, gray hair, and glasses stood behind it.

"Excuse me, but I'm not sure how to find anything about wolves and Germany."

He looked at me for a few minutes. I guess he never dealt with anyone as pale as me. I smiled at him to ease any tension.

"There was an article in the Global Post I read about problems with wolves. We have several news posts from all over the world. Here let me find that article for you.

Apparently, they hadn't had a problem with wolves for a while and now it came back with a vengeance."

He led me toward a section that had file boxes on shelves, according to the country they came from. He took the one down from Germany and took out the Global Post with the article in question.

"Here it is. I think you'll find this quite interesting. I know I did."

"Thank you for your help."

I took it back to where I had sat and leafed through it until I came upon the article, Germany has a serious wolf problem and no one knows what to do about it. The original article was published on April 27, 2014. Ok, now I'm headed in the right direction. I continued further;

SPREMBERG, Germany — Surrounded by a flock of 250-odd black-faced sheep near this northeastern town, Frank Neumann jams his green Trilby hat on his head before a gust of wind sends it flying, then chuckles as his 120-lb sheepdog leaps up to lick his face.

The bearlike Pyrenean mountain dog is people-friendly, but it's no pet. Before the stocky farmer obtained six of them to protect his flock, he arrived one morning to find 27 of his cherished sheep eviscerated, their guts strewn across the pasture. It was a tough way to learn that the wolf had returned to Germany. (Overdorf, Jason/Lifestyle & Beliefs/PRI/December 12, 2014)

Could Vanessa be one of these wolves? I delved deeper and found yet another interesting find entitled; Sex and Full Moon.

Jack pot! It went on to say that it was a known fact that in nature, for some animal species, the mating takes place during a full moon. They got that right.

As I read further, it went into the human race, male and female and the significance of sex and the full moon. My find was short lived, but I did read that a full moon lasts between four to five days.

"Guess Blood Moon will be my night place for a while."

After spending a good hour or two there, I went back to my house. I needed to find out where their boundary started, so I invited a few of my Domencio members over for some midnight fun and told them to bring *their own food.*

My guest was a young, voluptuous female who I met at the library, Cassandra Philips. She had red hair, long and her style was on the gothic side. Her name was Casandra.

I had wine glasses out, along with the best wine money could buy, hors d'oeuvres for our quest . . . little did they know they'd be our snacks.

Upon midnight, Casandra arrived first. She looked delicious. A small black tank top, with a netted jacket, black leather skirt, fish net stockings and black, wedge boots with spikes on the toes.

"Welcome Casandra, hope you found the place alright."

"This place is freaky. Way cool. This is your pad?" Her eyes roamed the walls, ceilings, and the foyer.

"Yes. Yes, this is my . . ." cleared my throat, "*pad* as you say. Come. I have wine and hors d'oeuvres."

I led her into the main room, she acted like a child in a candy shop. Everything seemed to fascinate her.

As the night crept along, others came. Laurent brought in his guest. A lovely black woman. Not too skinny, but plenty of meat on her. He liked her a lot I could tell. His hands were already seeking her out. Next to come in was Luther. Now, Luther has had a steady partner. I grew to like her as well. Her blood type was not to my liking, but it had qualities in it that reminded me of a dry red wine. Sweet.

"Hello, Natasha, so nice to see you again." It's customary

to kiss one's partner and Natasha was not the bashful kind. She pulled me in tight and gave me the full pleasure of her tongue. When through, she smiled and took Luther by the hand and up the stairs, they went. Natasha doesn't like to wait . . . for anything.

My last friend, Lafayette, my closest friend in our coven. He likes both the ladies and men. We, never, but others have. I've heard he is quite good in the bedroom.

"Lafayette my man! Who is this fine lady?" I took her hand and kissed it.

"This is Chantel. Chantel this is Jon."

"Pleasure. My, don't you look tempting."

"Why, are you from the south?" I asked.

"Why, yes. Yes, I am. Georgia, Alpharetta, Georgia."

"I've heard the ladies down south really know how to treat their men right? Is that correct?"

"Well, I don't know about that, but what I can say is this, you can help yourself any old time. Why I'd be pleased as punch if ya'll help yourself . . . together."

I looked at Lafayette. He didn't seem to mind, so I helped myself to a tiny bit of southern hospitality and kissed her.

Her lips were soft, succulent and oh, so tasty. Lafayette did well tonight.

"Lafayette, where have you been hiding this here lady. She is a keeper. If I were you, I'd hold onto this one tight."

She adjusted herself. Smiled sexy like and left with her arms clutched onto Lafayette.

Man, oh man, she could knock walls down with that wiggle of hers.

I had my friends place their partners in one room to socialize, while we went into the study to discuss business. I know, but business before pleasure.

"So, I've been asked to bring in the person whose been killing our Coven off and I have to say that I've found her . . ."

This brought on a flurry of banter among my fellow vampires, "but I need more information. For instance, they have a border, boundary line . . . where is it?"

Luther spoke first, "No one really knows for sure, but why need more information? You got her, bring her before Domencio to be killed."

If I told them my reasons they'd bring me before Domencio and then her. No, I had to come up with a lie, a well thought up one, one that couldn't fail. I'm good at that. Didn't take me long when I said, "She is their leader. If I brought her in to be killed, the rest of them would continue on without her. We'd be worse off than what we are now. No, we need to find where they are stationed. Where their sacred ground is and from there . . . *we* attack them."

I looked at their faces. Yes, my lie worked. Too well from what I saw.

"So, from I can see, we are all in agreement. Great! I believe the sooner the better. Domencio doesn't like to be kept waiting, especially when it comes to the Coven. Tomorrow we start, but for now, we have a room of lovely ladies. Ladies who are willing to provide us with refreshments. Let us be entertained."

---

10

*T*he next day I went to our Lair or as one would say, Domencio's house. He has a vast study with books and manuscripts that have far reaching information on all sorts of subjects. I thought it best to scout around and see what I could come up with, without anyone becoming suspicious of me.

Now our lair is a place that everyone in town proclaims it to be haunted. No one knows that in its depths is a crypt. It is hard to find, even if one knows about it. It is there that Domencio is laid.

The mansion is Victorian of course, built in 1874 and got its paranormal stories from past owners who have died there. It is also said, that the wife of the original owner roams the halls, wringing her hands, dressed in her mourning clothes. She is known in town as The Lady in Black. She mourns the death of her daughter and husband.

Many investigators who have come to see such sightings have claimed to have had such encounters. One felt her arm grow icy, cold that no coat would help and the urgency to leave became very demanding. Once outside, all such feeling and emotions vanished. Only when she'd gone back in, they were felt, but with more intensity.

So, with such stories going around, Domencio uses them to his advantage, as do the rest of us.

As for our monthly gatherings, no one ever sees us. They are held very late in the night when humans are asleep. No lighting is necessary, we have keen eye sight in the dark.

It's been in foreclosure since 2014. No one wants it because of the stories and investigations. Makes for the perfect place for us to live in.

The crypt is large, not small by any measure and with no windows, makes it ideal for us.

The walls and floor are cement with an ornate grate dead center. It has channels that lead to the center gargoyle, whose mouth is open, ready to take in its next nourishment.

It sort of reminds me of the grate in the movie Underworld, where victims are killed over it, letting the blood seep its way into the channels that awaken their master. I see its value and importance. Domencio is never awake unless need be.

It was late afternoon when I arrived. A few others were there, mostly in the front room, lounging about in the dark. It is one of my favorite rooms.

Dark velvet green draperies hung on the large, yet, ornate lead glass windows. Rococo style furniture, embellished with gold cording, filled the room as well. At the north side of the wall stood a renaissance oak chimney piece, its brass, and cast iron insert still gleamed as though it was recently placed. The best part of this hearth were the Atlanteans, one on either side, which looked as they held up the mantle themselves . . . my favorite piece.

I nodded to those who had the decency to look up and continued to the study.

With the door being wide opened, I saw no one else and

so I entered. Locked the door and searched the shelves for anything remotely close to werewolves. Wasn't all too sure I'd find anything, but I did come across a piece of paper. Folded, next to a book that read <u>Folklore of the Unforgiven.</u> Both intrigued me, but the paper proved more imperative. So I unfolded it.

Its paper quality was like parchment. A little more pliable, but nevertheless, it had been written many years ago.

Its language, again, pointed to that of German. There's the connection. The ink had a purple/black tone to it. I knew right away it was iron gall ink. It's made from iron salts and tannic acids from vegetable sources. It was the standard writing and drawing ink in Europe during the early 5th century.

Trinkwasser aus einem Wolfs-
Pfotenabdruck
Essen Wolf Gehirn
Tragen eines Wolfskin / Gürtels
Strumpfbandes
Werewolf's Bite
Ein Pakt mit dem Teufel
Familienfluch

This was a list of the different ways of becoming a werewolf. Where this would fit in with Vanessa I had no idea, but one of the ladies who wanted to rip my clothes off at the bar the other night spoke with an accent.

I needed another visit to the Blood Moon and I had only this week to do it.

11

*M*y buddies met up with me at one of my hockey games. I don't remember the other team's name, just remember they played decently. We were also evenly matched strength wise so we got our work cut out for us. On sided games bore me to death. It's like why even bother playing.

After the game, shower and got my gear all packed we went to check out Blood Moon together. Thought they could use some entertainment. Plus, they could see for themselves just how these shifters acted.

As always, I parked my vehicle down the street. We got out . . .

"Are you kidding me? Look at this place! It's crazy man and that line to get in!"

"Forget about the line, look at the ladies! Oh my God, they're beautiful and look at that one, she isn't wearing any panties under that short, short skirt." Lafayette's mouth had drool dripping from its corners.

"Gentlemen, ease up on the testosterone, will you. They

may be sexy ladies, but they're wolves, we aren't and we smell."

"We don't smell, they do! But I'm willing to forego that just to get a piece of some of that ass!"

They all started to grind their hips and moan with pleasure. Had to stop this quick or we'd all be doomed.

"Will you listen up? I hear what you're saying, but if we go in there we're dead meat. Put this on first."

I threw them some of my aftershaves and told them to lay it on heavy. Then, I told them we couldn't just walk in with the rest of them. They knew what I meant right away. No sooner did Luther layered on the scent, he vanished, as did the others and myself.

We all sat in a dark corner. The smell of horniness and sex lay thick in the air. My boys were all excited. Took all I could to get them to play it cool. We weren't one of them.

A waitress came up to our table and introduced herself as Saoirse. There was nothing left to the imagination in what she wore. She was gifted with assets.

"Hello boys, what'll it be tonight? Thirsty, hungry or both?"

"Hello Saoirse, for now, we'd like the best bottle of wine money can buy. That'll be all."

"You sure that's all you want? I can offer you more. My boss is all about the specials."

Luther couldn't hold back, but he controlled himself very well.

"I'd like a special if you don't mind? I've got a *load* that needs spending."

"I'm sure you do honey. I'm sure you do and I'd be more than happy to meet those needs. Just let me get your drinks first, then I'll give you your special."

Her walk had a little more energy to it as she turned.

Luther wasn't going to be able to walk tonight and she probably won't be breathing.

I looked at him. "You can't kill her. You know that don't you. If you do, it's not going to sit well with them. Let her have her way with you and vice versa, but no drinking her blood. Got that?"

With everyone in agreement, the night should go smoothly.

Saoirse came back with our wine and glasses and took Luther by the hand and off they went. Before he got out of his chair, she was on him.

"What kind of place is this a bar or a brothel?"

"It's a bar Laurent, but one that doesn't mind having orgies. Why don't you go out on the dance floor? I'm sure some horny wolf will find you appealing."

He more or less shrugged his shoulders, got up and walked over to the floor. Immediately he was taken with not one, but two ladies, both ready to go and Laurent seemed more than happy to give what they wanted.

"What about Lafayette? Don't you want some action?"

"Not now."

Something was wrong. Lafayette loved the ladies as did they, but something about him confused me.

"You can tell me, what's going on?"

"Don't you feel it? There's some bad blood going on here, bad blood. You were right in telling us not to drink. Yeah, it's bad."

"Get Luther, I'll find Laurent. Then, we'll leave. Don't wait for me, just go."

We split. I headed in the direction that Saoirse went. I thought it might be tricky. This place, though small from the outside was quite large on the inside.

I found a hallway with doors on both sides.

Must be the rooms they have sex in. I thought.

"What the hell . . ." and opened the first one I came too.

I was right. A couple looks like she was well pleased with her choice. Quite hung from the looks of things.

"Oh, sorry, my mistake. Carry on."

"They just looked at me, not even stopping."

Ok. On to the next door.

As you may have guessed, more sex, this time a threesome and they wanted to make it a foursome, with me!

"Looks pretty crowded already. Rain check?" And shut the door.

"Damn, where is Laurent?"

I had checked all the rooms and hadn't found him. There was one more door, at the end of the hall I hadn't opened. This one led outside. I had a bad feeling about this one.

I stepped out and hear noises, moans. I kept on, in the direction from where they came from and sure enough, I found him. He was on top of Saoirse, giving his all and got himself so worked up, he went into vampiric mode.

"Don't bite!" I screamed.

He stopped. Looked at me. His eyes weren't red, they were yellow. Something I hadn't seen before.

He snarled and hissed at me. Protective of his prey. He wasn't going to share. He was all predator now, Laurent wasn't there in him.

"Laurent, it's me Jon, your buddy. It's time to go."

Saoirse was still alright, but scared. She already saw his fangs and knew she made a mistake. Surprised she didn't shift into her wolf form and attack him, which led me to believe that maybe she wasn't a shifter, just a waitress.

"Saoirse, are you a shifter?"

"W-what's that?"

Ok, got my answer. "Never mind love, have fun."

I walked away. Laurent, after seeing me leave, gave one last thrust, then bit down . . . hard. She jerked once.

I didn't want to stay. She'd be missed and someone would come out to look for her. Laurent made a mistake. I warned him. Now, it would be up to him to save his own skin.

12

*L*uther and Lafayette were in the car waiting for me.

"You guys ok?"

"Where's Laurent? Did you find him?" Luther asked.

"Yeah, I found him. He was nailing Saoirse outside, in the back parking lot."

They whooped it up and gave each other high fives, but when they saw my face they went still.

"What happened Jon?"

"Laurent killed her. Don't worry, she wasn't a shifter, but that puts us in danger. Someone is going to find her and they're going to know a vampire had done it. Damn him. I warned him not to do drink from anyone, little lone kill! He put us in a predicament. Domencio will need to know."

"But if you tell Domencio, he'll want Laurent burned."

"I can't help that. He screwed not only her but us as well. It's got to be done. If you see him, bring him to me. I'll deal with it."

A frenzy had already begun as we left. Screams were

heard and people rushed out, shifted as they did. They wanted us.

They must have caught our scent. A few of them ran in our direction. I had the pedal down to the floor, cursing as I maneuvered around tight curves. I had to get us back to the lair. Had to warn Domencio.

"Luther, leave the car. Go straight to Domencio and awaken him. We need to get as many of us together as possible. Go!"

Without hesitation, Luther was gone. He soared above the town, through alleys and narrow streets till he came to the lair. Upon, entering, he headed down to the crypt.

To enter, you must say a few words. The wall is ornate with a carved beast biting down on a female victim. To anyone else it would appear to be a decorative wall, but behind it lay death.

"În timpul nopții, pe fiara înaripată, sărbătoarea începe când se trezește."

Rumbling and grinding, the wall itself had opened. A whoosh of cold, stale air rushed out and there, in the darkness, light. Torches burned on either side of what looked like a throne, while gargoyles sat on either side of the arm rests. There, on the floor, just in front of it were channels that stretched across till it came to the center of the room, where it was met with more channels. They wound themselves into a tight coil, ending up at a mouth near the center of it all.

Luther stood at the foot of the throne, where the channel started and slit his wrist. The blood dripped down into the channel and made its way through the coils, entering the mouth. There, when entered, clanging started in and the grate rose, till it was, in height, six feet.

It was a glass capsule of sorts and inside, an emaciated creature stood. Dead, but on the cusp of being woken.

Luther knew where he should stand and not by the throne. His place is the entrance, where he first came in.

The capsule, creaked and moaned its way toward the throne and stopped. It turned and the door to it opened. Luther couldn't see anything, but within minutes giant, bat like wings, leathery in appearance and moist, stretched out on either side, then disappeared.

"Who has woken me?" Came a voice, low and deep.

"It is I, Luther, my Lord. I bring urgent news."

"What is it?"

"Laurent has killed a human . . ."

"And this is the urgency you wake me on? A death of a human?"

"Sir, she with the shifters. They're on their way here. They're mad and seek revenge."

Domencio huffed. "Mad indeed. Brainless animals that they are. Go tell the others and bring Laurent to me."

13

*L*uther fled the crypt, up the stairs and into the front room and was met with Jon and Lafayette. Together they called everyone to listen.

"Domencio has called on us to battle. The shifters are on their way. They seek revenge." Warned Luther.

"Revenge, for what? We've done nothing!"

"Listen to him, he's telling the truth!" I told them.

"Laurent has killed a human. One that worked for them at the Blood Moon."

"What do they care? It's not like she was one of them. She's a human! Good for Laurent!"

"No, you don't understand, she was the owner's lover."

This brought on a whole new outlook on the impending battle. They all took to the outside, out of sight and waited. Luther, on the other hand, went to look for Laurent.

"Don't! Luther! Stay here. I think I know where he might have . . ."

Out of the darkness, an echoing sound grew louder and louder. The shifters closed in.

They appeared seconds later, about 20 or so. Big, mad,

and ready to kill we took our stance from above and attacked.

Being quick and agile, it wasn't hard to battle shifters. They were big, brawny and bulky, made moving quickly at a disadvantage to a point.

Animals and vampires were flung left to right, while the sound of breaking bones and necks filled the air. We weren't outnumbered, but both sides had loses. It didn't end there.

Domencio had his digs in as well. His form was nothing they were ready for. He was first and foremost a dangerous creature. Bat like in some ways, devilish in others. His wing spanned stretched out eight feet on either side of him and on the tips of each wing, a dagger like appendage struck with such force that it had no trouble breaking through an old Oak tree that stood behind one of the shifters. Impaled it as it were.

Domencio then, as the shifter hung, limp with terror etched on its face, slit him wide open with his teeth. Blood and insides fell to the ground with a splat.

With much pleasure and disgust, he released the shifter and went on to kill at least five more. All met their doom in the same gruesome end.

We took our dead to the crypt, there Domencio met with us all. I, in the meantime, had found Laurent and brought him with me.

Domencio, though gaunt in stature, proved himself tonight. He sat there, on his chair and glared at us and those whose lives were senselessly killed. His anger would show no mercy.

"Laurent, come forward."

He knew he was done for. His body shivered out of fear for his life and fell to his knees and begged for mercy.

"SILENCE!"

"You have brought shame to our Coven. You have lost us

members of our coven. This is punishable by *death*. TIE HIM DOWN!!"

Marcus and Draven grabbed his arms and tied him to the grate on the floor. The same grate that brought forth Domencio himself.

"Please my lord. I met no harm. She isn't one of them! She's human! I did nothing wrong!"

"Quiet! I need to know more. Jonathan, what say you?"

Now, I'm not one to scare easily, as you well know, but answering to Domencio is another thing. He made me who I am. I am the son he never had. So, you see now, I should be given as much respect as he, but I don't. Doesn't bother me, unless, something like this happens and puts my butt on the line.

"Laurent, along with Luther and Lafayette, went to the Blood Moon. It's a club for shifters. You did want me to find the shifter who had been killing off our members and I was told she'd be there."

"Go on."

"Well, it being a full moon, things were intense there . . ."

"Yes, I am well aware of the full moon and the effects it has. Make your point."

"Laurent found this waitress, Saoirse, tempting and allowed herself to be taken. I warned him though. The others can vouch for me. He didn't listen. He became obsessed with her and couldn't control himself. He turned into . . ." I looked over at him, "into something I hadn't seen before. It was as if his true self as a vampire changed. That's when he killed her."

Domencio looked at Laurent, then gave the signal. Marcus held within his hand a silver sword. He held it high and in one fell swoop off went Laurent's head. Draven then took the torch from off the wall and ignited the remains. It took but seconds.

"Leave us alone. I wish to talk to my son."

I stood there. Not knowing what my Father wanted, but I knew it wouldn't be good.

"Jonathan come here."

I walked over to where he sat and knelt before him. Even though he was my father, I still humbled myself to him.

"My lord."

"When you first came to me you were awkward, scared, but I knew you better. I knew that within time, you would learn from me and become something I could be proud of."

Out of the blue, a flash of white light and pain struck my face. I found myself on my back ten feet from where I knelt. The right side of my face burnt. Blood coated my hand from where I felt. I looked at my Father, the tenderness had gone from his eyes.

"You have made a *fool* of me. This could have been avoided. Death could have been avoided had you taken better control of Laurent. He was one of the strongest if not the best vampire I had beside you . . . now I have *nothing* . . . NOTHING!"

His wings expanded outwardly, as he soared to the ceiling. His demonic face, snarled as the rapier like ends, stabbed through my shoulders and lifted me upward with him.

"YOU HAVE LOST ME ONE OF MY OWN! For this, you will be punished."

As his wings opened wider, so did the wounds on my shoulders. Bone and ligaments cracked under the strain and I was sent crashing to the floor. I couldn't move.

"Leave my sight. You are a disgrace to me."

I got to my feet out of sheer will power. The use of my arms was gone, though the healing process had begun. Every move sent bolts of pain which shot through my body. Death would have been easier to handle than this. I realized why he chose this method and accepted it.

14

*L*aid up on the couch, I felt pissed. I lost my friend and partner. It was my fault. I knew that now. Shit.

A knock at the door took me out of my stupor. "Come in!"

Silence.

"I said, oh, forget it. Hang on."

I got up and went to the door. Now, the usage of my arms wasn't too bad, but it wasn't great either, so it took some time to grasp the door knob and turn. Opening was a whole different pain.

"Vanessa, come to finish me off?"

"No, but you did say, that the next time we met up, I should listen to my body language."

I didn't want to deal with this now, even though a part of me wanted her, but I could push that away. I, unlike others in my coven, can control my urges.

I sauntered back to my couch and plopped down. "Have a seat." I motioned with a wave of my arm.

"My, aren't we gallant. You treat all ladies with such charm?"

"I did offer a chair what more do you want?" I closed my eyes to wish her away.

"My, we are in a mood today. What cat got your tongue or should I say . . . wolf?"

That was the straw that broke the camel's back. I sat up so fast she didn't have time to breathe.

"I lost a good friend of mine yesterday. I don't care about manners right now, especially to the likes of you."

"I lost some friends myself. I'm not happy about it, but I'm here."

"You want a medal or something?"

"I can see this isn't a good time, maybe I should . . ."

"You think?" I got up and walked over to the window. It was cloudy and gray. Exactly how I felt.

She came over to me. Stood quietly. I didn't say anything, didn't want to. I looked over at her. Her eyes were closed, as if, in meditation. God, she was beautiful. I kept my eyes on her. It had been about five minutes, maybe more before she opened them, then smiled at me.

"You were right."

Then walked out.

I didn't go after her, I didn't have to. She knew, as did I. We connected, but why? Our species don't get along. Never have, never will, but there's something between us. We would meet again. When I didn't know, but it would be soon.

A few days had gone by. The use of my arms was back to normal. Every day I'd go to the exercise room at the college to build them back up, not that I needed to, vampires don't lose their strength. It did give me something to do, however. I've been rather depressed about Laurent.

The other day I saw the girl he had brought to my house. She was beautiful. Dark, chocolate skin, deep, brown eyes and thick lips, soft and warm. I didn't want to talk to her. I knew if I had she'd asked about Laurent and I couldn't tell her. It's like opening an old wound.

As I finished up, I saw Vanessa outside. She was alone and saw me. I still didn't want to talk, but I couldn't stay away completely, we had things to discuss.

"Hey, how are you feeling? Any better?"

"Why are you being so nice to me anyway? I thought you hated me."

"Hate is such a strong word, loathed would be better."

I went to turn away when she caught my arm.

"Stop. I'm sorry. Look, I felt something the other night, the night I first sensed you at the Blood Moon, I felt that connection then. It scared me."

"You felt it then?"

"Yeah, I did. I didn't want to say anything to you because . . . well, we're not supposed to get along, but here we are. Makes no sense."

"You're right, it doesn't. Look, you want to get some coffee or something? I know a great place, just outside of town."

"Alright. I could use a good cup."

We got into my car and drove 30 miles south to a small café called, Frankies. Not much to look at, but it had the best coffee. Now, vampires aren't the type to drink anything but wine, but I'm not your typical vampire. I don't eat a lot. I like things to be on the rare side. Vegetables are more my style.

I held the door open for her as we entered and sat at a booth in the far corner.

"So, what do you think?"

"Well, it's not much to look at, but it does smell good inside. Sort of reminds me of the 50s."

"You're not that old are you?"

"No! I've seen pictures of places like this."

"What will it be?" The waitress said as she came up to our

table. She seemed to be about in her late 50s. Thick waistline, glasses, graying hair.

"Two coffees, cream, and sugar."

She wrote it down and turned away to get our order. In minutes she was back with two cups and filled them to the top.

"Cream and sugar are already on your table. Enjoy folks."

We fixed our coffees. Vanessa has a unique way of doing hers. Almost like a method. First, she pours in the cream, stirs, then adds the second creamer, stirs again, tastes, then the final touches a dab of sugar and gives it one last stir.

"Do you do that all the time?" I asked.

"Yeah, why? Does it bother you?"

"No, it's just . . . never mind. So, tell me about yourself, your family life."

She held her cup between her two hands and sipped. It wasn't until she took another sip that she began to talk.

"I was an only child, which I didn't mind. I didn't need a play mate, my mother and father were all I wanted. It wasn't until I turned 6 that things got bad." She paused for another sip. "My parents weren't getting along and they fought often. One day it got so bad that my father left us and never came back."

"I'm sorry."

"No, don't. Mother and I were alright alone. We didn't need anyone else to make our lives happy. One night though, my mother met someone outside while she hung the laundry. I didn't meet him until a few days later when she invited him in for tea."

Invited . . . "Were you already a shifter?"

"Yes. Why do you ask?"

"Nothing. Go on." I drank my coffee as she continued.

"I was in my bedroom, taking a nap. I remember as if it were yesterday, the nightmare. It came on so sudden. I couldn't wake up. I dreamt that a creature chased me up a hill and then caught me. He held me in his clutches and . . . and . . ." she turned to me, "and bit my neck. I remember being sick for the next few days, or maybe it was weeks, I can't remember."

"Vanessa . . ."

"Don't say it. Please don't. My mother, she was afraid. She too was bitten"

"This wasn't a dream Vanessa, it really happened!"

"The pack got wind of the attack. We couldn't stay. We no longer belonged. We were outcasts. So, we packed up our stuff and left, but one member was mad. He felt that we should have been killed, but our pack leader said it wasn't our fault and chided him for his anger. A couple days later, at night, he came to our house, the wolf in our pack. I hid under the bed like my mother told me too and not come out. I waited and waited, for what seemed like hours and when I felt it safe to come out, that's when I saw her. She was on the floor, dead in a pool of blood."

"Vanessa stop. You don't have to tell me everything."

"But I do . . . for days I kept to myself. Hunted only at night. One night, during winter, another pack had come by the house. They sensed I was alone and took me under their wing. That's where I am today."

"Vanessa, you understand now why we connect. You're part vampire."

"I know."

"Tell me something, why have you been killing members of my coven, especially when you're one of us?"

"I felt I had to, for my pack. That, and I hated who I was. It was because of a vampire that I lost my mother."

"No, a vampire didn't kill your mother, your own kind did."

"Because of a vampire."

"What are you going to do?"

"I don't know. We can't be seen together, not like this. It's too dangerous."

"Vanessa, I've been ordered to hunt you down and bring you before Domencio. He wants to kill you."

"What? I have to go. I can't be here. Good bye."

She rushed out into the night. I didn't go after her. She was right. I had to figure this out. Taking her before Domencio was no longer in the plan.

15

I went home. The event between Vanessa and I wouldn't stop. It replayed itself over and over again. The look on her face when she told me her story. The fright on her face, when I told her I'd been ordered to hunt her down. I had a lot to think about and not much time.

After I left Jonathan I went back to my apartment.

I unlocked the door and just stood there. Numb. My nightmare that I had pushed and locked away had come back to haunt me. How could I have just ignored what I knew one day would surface? I thought if I ignored it enough, I'd forget that it even happened. That I could have a normal life within my new family. For the most part, I did. Little did I realize that at some point I'd have to come to terms with it.

I had a game to play. A late game, 11:30 p.m. I needed to bust some bones. Take my frustrations out on a few guys. Wouldn't fix the situation any, but I'd forget about it for a while. I know that doesn't sound like I'm handling this well . . . I'm not, but I couldn't sit and dwell on it either. That would be worse than anything.

All during the game, my thoughts kept going back to Vanessa, then Domencio.

BAM!

Checked into the side boards, on my ass.

Son of a bitch! The dude, dead in my books. I hauled ass. He had the puck. It was gonna be mine in a few short seconds.

With my stick lifted high, I swept in a downward motion, catching his blade and down he went.

TWEET!

Penalty. Tripping.

My stomach felt sour. So, I put on the kettle to make some hot tea. Went into my room and put on my sweat pants, baggie sweater, and slippers. My comfort clothes.

Twenty minutes later, the kettle called out and I got a cup and placed my favorite tea bag in . . . Constant Comment. The smell as soon as the hot water hit the bag brought immediate relief. No more did I think about Jon or anything else. I would just sit on my couch, feet up with a blanket and sip my tea.

No sooner did I get comfortable, someone knocked on the door.

Two-minute penalty. The game was still zero to zero. We were evenly matched. Patrick, tall, lanky dude, had the puck. Not a fast skater, but he had gotten better since that first game. He just crossed the blue line when out of the blue the opponent came from behind and knocked the puck away. Damn.

Finally, my penalty had ended. It was a change on the fly and I had less than a minute to score before the period ended.

Their team was at our end. Tom and one of their players were battling it out for the puck. I aided in the process. Didn't have time for any quien es mas macho.

I made a beeline straight for them, stuck my stick in and got the puck, then rounded around their net, out the side and down to their end.

Now, who was it? Please let it not be the girls."Hey, why aren't you dressed for tonight? It's the last day of the full moon?"

Em, my closest friend. She loved to party. I usually did too, but not tonight. Didn't want any guy touching me, or even look at me. The whole thing nauseated me.

"I don't feel like it Em. I think I'll just stay at home if you don't mind."

"I do mind! What's wrong with you? You're usually the one to get us going and stuff, now you've done an about face. What's up with that?"

She looked great as always. I didn't want her to miss out on her last night of yummy men. As, much as I didn't feel like it, I agreed.

"Oh, that's my girl! Come on. The guys are going to be hotter than ever tonight. Maybe you'll find your soulmate. No?" Her eyes held that glimmer of hope, but shot mine down instantly.

I didn't need to find my soulmate. I found him, but I wouldn't let her know.

There I was, skating as if my life depended on it. People were cheering, others yelling, it was my time. A perfect break away.I used my strength to get me down to their end faster and to hit that puck in. It was like a dream. Just me and the puck, soaring down, ready to make that score. Crossing the center line, I neared their goal. The goalie not sure where I would strike teetered from side to side, readying himself for my move.

As I skated nearer he skated back. Closing the gap between him and the net. That didn't stop me. I'd get it in with a fake to the left, then hit it into the right.

SCORE!

Blood Moon was packed. The hormones were at an all-time high and no one held back. I often wondered at times why any of them wore clothes.

I had a small leather skirt on, tight top and black stilettos. Provocative enough, but not slutty. I didn't want to attract anyone, not tonight, but it was hard not to. There were some hunky wolves out there on the floor.

Em, as soon as she stepped foot inside the men were on her. Yeah, hormones were flying.

"Hey, sexy, what do you say you and I hit the dance floor? I bet you got some really nice moves, especially after seeing your cute little ass."

"You think so huh? Why not, you're not so bad yourself."

We got out on the floor. The music had a good, grinding beat to it. Got his juices going. His hands were all over me. Normally this wouldn't bother me at all, but tonight, they made me feel dirty.

"Watch it," I said in tones that meant business.

"Oh, hard to get huh? I like that. Makes things spicy. Come on girl, let's see what you got under that skirt of yours."

He cornered me against the wall. I let him continue till I could get him at his weakest position and then let him have it.

"Oh baby, you're so soft. Mmm . . . I just want to see you scream for more."

He placed his leg between mine, then his hands started up my skirt.

Show time . . .

"Oh, yeah, you want me do you? How about I make you scream for more? Would you like that sugar?"

He just smiled and ground his hips into mine, that's

where I made my move. I soccer punched him right in the groin then held on tight. I call it my death grip.

"Scream baby, scream. Let mama hear you good and loud."

He screamed and loud. No one paid attention. Damn, the music was so loud and everyone else was too busy screwing to see that I held a man's life in my little hand.

"Next time you want a piece of me, you act like a gentleman. You got that?" My grip got tighter, then I let go. He fell to the floor in a fetal position.

"One point for me, zero for you."

After the game, I did my usual, shower, packed my gear and headed home, though I didn't want to. Something ate at my insides. I had to see Vanessa.

I left the place. Told Em to just stay and have fun and that I'd call her tomorrow. Tonight I had to go somewhere. Had to see someone . . . Jonathan.

I headed toward the college. Don't know why I just needed to go there. I parked in the J parking lot, got out, and saw someone by the entrance . . . Vanessa.

She saw me and started to walk over. Our eyes never left each other. Closer and closer, until we stood there. Inches apart.

"Hello," I said.

"Hello."

That was it, nothing more. Next, we were in each other's arms. Embraced in a love that wasn't met to be, yet, felt so perfect. So right.

I awoke in a ghost like mist, confused and dazed, not sure what had just happened and I was in pain, though I had no wounds.

As minutes passed, my whereabouts became clearer and I found myself outside in a parking lot . . . at Frankie's.

"What the hell?"

Getting up proved to be a challenge. It felt as though my guts would spill out.

I remembered Vanessa and I had coffee there and that we were making amends or so I thought. Then I recalled our conversation. She talked about her mother and how a vampire had bitten them. Her mother died and she killed members of my coven because of that, but she's one of us. She's partially one of us, the other, a shifter.

"Shit . . . I told her I had to bring her in, but . . ."

Searing pain this time erupted.

"Damn . . . we hugged, we . . . no . . . it couldn't, it —

It was just a dream. I didn't play a game, nor did . . . Vanessa . . . I saw what she dreamt. I got to get my hands on that shifter that got his dirty hands on my mate, but wait . . . how could I see into her dreams?

"Our connection."

Buckled in pain, I fell to the ground. I had to get home. I had to find her. Had to tell her I wouldn't bring her in, but . . ."

Get to your feet man. I told myself, then it dawned on me. The connection again . . .

"Damn, she's hurt!"

When I arrived at my house, the gate was opened as was my front door. Any of my covens was welcomed in anytime whether I'm there or not, but I would know they were there.

The pain seemed to ease up, but that didn't ease my mind, for if it were the case, she didn't have long.

I had a secret entrance that I used for just such occasions and without hesitation, I entered through its passage.

This passage I had a contractor make and from the outside, you can't see it, but if you knew of it and went looking for it, you'd probably find it. It's a bit tricky, sometimes even for me when I've fed on too much blood. Excitability tends to leave me thick, not often, but at times.

The entrance leads you into a dark room. No lights and rather dank, as moisture tend to build on the walls. Great torture room if you ask me, but I'm not into such things. Just kill and be done with it. Though some of our members love the dramatics. They get off on it. Childish really, besides, I have better class than to play with my food.

I reached the first level. You enter into the kitchen from it. Immediately it hit me . . .

"Vanessa!"

Nothing.

She was upstairs . . . the last room on the left, just past mine. I found her on the floor, bloodied and barely breathing. She lay face down, her clothes were ripped beyond recognition, and her skin looked as though someone tried to open her up. In that, her back had a deep, long gash down the middle, with bits of torn flesh dangling from the wound. Legs, arms, and neck had been slashed, while her face . . . thank God, didn't get too bad of a beating. Her eyes were swollen shut, but that was it. Bad enough though.

"Who did this to you?"

I had to get her off the floor. The bed wasn't that far and so carefully, without causing too much pain, turned her over. A muffled moan sounded.

"I know. I know. I'm sorry, but I have to move you. Just bear with me for just a few minutes, then I promise you, I won't touch you."

As I rolled her over gently, I saw that her front was just as bad as her back.

She let out a scream as back connected with the hard floor. Somehow, I had to pick her up and get her to the bed, but I didn't know how without adding to the pain. Not a spot on her was left unharmed.

"Ok, this will probably hurt, but I have to put you on the bed. You'll thank me."

Slow and easy, I snaked my right arm under her neck as my left arm went under her knees, then I began to lift . . .

"MY BACK!" She screamed.

I kept going. Her body shook with spasms while shrieks reverberated off the walls.

As gently as I could, I placed her on the bed . . . unhurriedly and even at that, she still cried out. I was furious at what was done to her.

Luther came in.

"What happened to her?" He came closer.

"She had been attacked, by who I don't know and where I'm not sure of that either. They hadn't been a struggle that I could tell around here or in the house.

"Do you think her own pack had done this to her?"

"No, why should they? They don't usually attack another member unless they did something against them."

"Maybe they found out about you."

That sounded plausible, but we were always alone, so who would have known. Then, out of the blue . . . "Here friends saw me talking to her at the college."

"That's it. They attacked her. But I think it's better that they got to her first. Domencio would've had her reduced to ashes."

My hand, clutched the front of his shirt, as he soared up and out of the room. Before he even had a chance to evaporate, we were at it again, vampire to vampire. Didn't matter if we were in the same coven, he over stepped his boundary.

"You are going against Domencio . . . for a . . . *wolf*. I can see that she's a good piece of ass, but if that were me, that's all she'd be good for. Maybe a sip or two, but that's it. She's a wolf. A stinking, four, legged, and a tail animal. What's even worse, she's killed off some of our own kind, from out lair. Get it together or else."

I didn't bust him up too bad, but enough to get my point across, but it did have a point. I was going against my own kind. Vampire, wolf, you just don't do that . . . ever. If you do, either or both wind up dead for crossing the line.

I wanted to ask him, what he would do if someone went after his soulmate, what would he do, but I already knew the answer. He'd never go outside his race. The thing is, he didn't know that she too, was half vampire and he never will.

I went downstairs, locked the front door, shut the curtains and went back upstairs. I stayed there . . . for days on end.

*W*olves heal, like us, but not as fast, though she is part us, it hadn't been enough. Good thing I don't need to sleep, though I can. Every moan, cry or whimper, I stayed close to her side, even laid next to her, but didn't do that too often, any movement made her wince in pain.

A couple of weeks had gone by. She'd been improving on a daily basis, still not taking anything to drink or eat. Sleep seemed to be the only thing she wanted most.

I made sure her face was washed and tended to her wounds daily. A doctor or nurse was out of the question, besides what she was, was good enough medicine around. I just made sure they were kept cleaned and bandaged.

Which brings me to a story. I had to go to the store to get more gauze and ointment. I knew going in, that aside from my pale, sickly look, but refined features, I was loaded down with bandages. The thoughts were right on the money at times, other times they thought it was for me and felt sorry for me. Other's thought I had cancer. One old lady, the kind with the Grandma cheeks, all rosy, bluish, with tinted, bluish hair and smelled of roses, that kind. She came over with this sad look on her face and gave me a hug and said, "God bless you."

I didn't know what to say, so I gave her a smile and exited out the door. Good thing I got a lot, I don't think I could do that again.

When I arrived home, Vanessa sat upright in her bed. She looked a bit worn out, pale and thin, but more alert than she had been in a long time.

"Well, look at you! How do you feel?" I set my bag on the chair and sat down next to her.

"I look like shit. I feel like shit. What did you get?" As she eyed the bag.

I went to the medical store. You needed more supplies. I got a hug from an old lady. She blessed me.

Her eyebrow raised in a question mark.

"She *hugged* you. Did you compel her to do that?"

"No! She felt sorry for me and gave me a hug and said, God, bless you. It was all very touching, but I had to get out of there. It was too much for me.

Vanessa tried to laugh, but grabbed her sides instead and huffed a few times. That was her way of laughter. She's improving!

"Sorry for you. Why? Because you looked so pathetic that she thought you needed one?"

"Something like that. I heard what people were saying. Some thought I had cancer, others thought I had some sort of disease . . . it proved that there is still hope for mankind."

"Why would you care what mankind thinks? You killed them for nourishment."

Let's not get testy, shall we? Remember who nursed you back to health."

"Well, I'm not that healthy, at least, not yet, but thank you just the same. It was sweet of you to do all this."

"What did you want me to do, leave you on the floor and die?"

She paused for a moment. "How did I get here? I don't remember."

"Vanessa, do you remember who attacked you?"

Again, she paused for thought. Eyes closed winced some . . .

"I don't . . . I don't remember. I think I was almost home or was home when I got knocked down from behind, then before I could get up . . . another blow . . . that's all I remember, but . . . did you bring me here?"

I was incredulous. She didn't know.

"Sweetheart . . . "

"Don't call me that."

"Ok, Vanessa, I found you on the floor, here in my bedroom."

She looked away. Her hands clutched the bedding as her eyes closed once more.

"Vanessa?'

"I need to sleep. I-I'm tired." Then sank down into the bed and curled up.

"Alright. We'll talk after you've rested."

She said nothing, so I left. She knew something. I felt it. I couldn't read her thoughts this time. She shut me out. For being on death's door, she still held on to her craftiness. Fine, but she will tell me. I wouldn't press her.

18

I had to find out who had done this to her. We hadn't spoken since last night and the more she kept quiet, the more stressed I got. Stress and I don't do well. I am not the suave, debonair man when I'm like that. Those are the times I hate the most. I like being charming, cunning, sly . . . this – this was murder.

I thought about hanging with the guys, but since my last encounter with Luther, I thought that I should stay clear from him . . . all of them in fact. Hockey seemed like a good idea, but we didn't have a game, not until next week. The college was out as well. Her friends . . . no, I think the college is a good idea. Maybe they'll let something slip out. College it was.

I went upstairs. I'd been staying downstairs to give her space, but I needed to change. She'd just have to deal with it.

I came into the room. Not quietly either. I had, had enough being Nurse Nanny and I wanted my house back. I know I should be more supportive and I had been, but I can only deal with so much.

She was up when I came in.

"Would it kill you to knock before entering?"

"Why should I? It's my room." And went to my closet.

"I could have been changing my clothes?"

I stuck my head out. Smiled.

"You, up and changing clothes? You have a hard time just sitting there, little lone getting up! Please . . ." And went back in.

"Still . . . !"

I came out, placed my clothes on the chair and begun to undress. I knew it would unnerve her, plus, I'm a man. I have needs. Undressing in front of a lady is sexy. How she dealt with it would be up to her.

"Do you mind?" Annoyed.

"It's my room, I can change my clothes if need be. Sorry, you happened to be here. Look away if it bothers you." And I kept on.

I loved her pout. Angry pout to be exact. Nevertheless, a pout. She didn't look away but watched. She was determined to prove me wrong.

I purposely went slowly. My eyes never left hers as I unsnapped, unzipped and pulled my pants down. I had briefs on. Tight, black ones, that left nothing to the imagination. Then, the shirt. They broke the mold after I was made. Good thing too, cause I don't think I could deal with another vampire who looked as good as me.

I could tell my little show had made things difficult for her. I planned it that way.

"Can you hurry up?" Her voice terse.

"Sorry, but these things take time. Can't rush greatness."

I walked toward her. Her eyes widened.

Sat on the edge of the bed. She moved away but would glance at my package. She wanted it bad.

"Sure I couldn't help you with anything before I go?"

Her legs crossed. Hands clutched and unclutched the sheets.

"Ah, no. I'm, a . . . I'm fine thank you." Cleared her throat.

"Sure? I mean, I don't mind if you need me for anything . . . *anything* at all."

"No, I'm fine. Just . . . just go and . . . just go."

"Alright then. I won't be gone long. Just don't go anywhere. Deal?"

"Where do you think I'm going to go? Dancing? Come on! Give me more credit than that."

I stood up, walked back to my clothes and got dressed. I emphasized how I zipped up my pants before putting on my shirt and shoes. She was hurting and not pain wise either. I was too, but she'd have me tonight. No doubt about that.

I walked out of my room. Closed the door behind me and waited. What I heard didn't surprise me. She got up, went straight to the bathroom and turned on the shower.

Oh yeah, I got to her. I thought. Haven't lost my touch.

I arrived at the college and sought out her friends. They were in the library this time. Good place. It's quiet and with the book shelves, they'd hide my presence from their view.

They were at the back middle tables. Their books were strewn about and papers in neat stacks laid in front of them. They weren't studying, just appeared that way. Explains a lot.

I parked myself on the other side of the book shelf that was directly next to them. From what I could hear, their conversation, at the moment was about classes, men and then Vanessa.

"I don't see why Charlotte had to take her to that stinking vampire's house. What did that prove?"

"It proved that we know what she's been up to and if that's the kind of person she wants, then will take her to him." Said Emily.

"Yeah, but she . . . I mean, why kill her?"

"Look, she broke the rules. She's lucky she didn't get killed. Charlotte did her a favor, by keeping her alive."

"Barely."

"Well, she had it coming."

So, some chick named Charlotte. Part of their park I take it. I'll have to follow them to see where this pack lived. That way, I'll also know where their boundary is.

They were there for another boring hour. What women talk about is garbage. When men have conversations, its intellectual stuff. History, news, sports . . . you know, interesting stuff. Women talk about shoes, clothes, and gossip about other women. My mind hurts.

Finally, they gathered their stuff and headed out the door. It would seem that they didn't drive. Instead, they walked. At least they were health conscience.

I followed them all the way to the edge of where the West side ends and the East side starts. The river! The river is where their territory started. Makes sense that Blood Moon would also be on the East side.

Now, to see where they all reside would be the next step. After we crossed the bridge, they continued for another three miles or so, until they came to an abandoned hospital.

Who'd of thought?

They entered through a window, whose boarding was taken off. I hadn't planned on going in, that would be suicide, but at least I knew where to go looking for them. I'd stake them out on a daily basis and find who this Charlotte person was. When I do, she's going to wish she never dealt with Vanessa.

I rushed to get home. I needed Vanessa and I knew she needed me. My muscles were already gearing up as I entered and ran up the stairs.

"I'm home, did you miss me?" As I entered the room. She wasn't there.

Frozen to my spot I listened. She was here. No one else. A sigh of relief.

"Vanessa? Where are you?"

"I'm downstairs. You ran past me."

She was in the front room. I went back down and found her on the couch with a blanket and a tray with hot tea and cookies.

"So, you have your appetite back. That's good and you're downstairs as well. Looks like you'll be good as new soon."

"You can say that. Actually, my wounds have healed up. Still somewhat sore, but I can deal with it. All I need now is to get my strength back up and I'll be on my way."

"You're leaving? You can't leave, they'll kill you for sure. No. I won't allow it."

"Won't allow it? You're not my father. I can do as I please. Just because you nursed me back to health, doesn't give you any reason to tell me what I can and cannot do."

"You're my soulmate. I *can* tell you what to do, especially if your life is in danger and it is."

"Who said I was your soulmate?"

"Our connection. Remember? It's why you ran away the first time and probably why you're here now."

She looked at me this time. Concerned.

"What are you getting at?"

"I know who did this and why?"

"You do? How?"

"Doesn't matter. What matters is that your own pack did this to you and brought you here because you broke their rules."

She didn't say anything. Stared at the tea tray, then the floor. Never at me. I knew her thoughts. She let me in.

"It's ok. You haven't done anything wrong, don't you see that? But, they can't know that you're part . . . vampire. They'll come after you and kill you."

She brought up her knees and wrapped her arms around them, while fingers laced together as she thought.

"Vanessa say something."

"What do you want me to say?"

"That you'll stay. You have to realize that's it's for the best."

This time she did look at me.

"I do know, but I'm not sure."

"Don't be afraid. I understand your fear. I'm scared too."

"Oh, stop. Since when have you ever been scared?"

"When I saw you ripped to shreds weeks ago, laying on my bedroom floor. I thought you were dead. Tell me something . . . why did they tear you open like they did? Were they trying to kill you?"

She didn't look at me when she spoke. Almost embarrassed from the look of things.

"When . . ." pause . . . "to see if a human is a werewolf or not, one slice into the skin to see if hair is revealed or not. If hair is revealed then they are one, if not . . ."

"Did they find any?"

Her eyes looked up at me . . . I didn't need words to tell me they didn't.

"But you are one though!"

"I shift into a wolf, doesn't make me a werewolf. I don't change when there is a full moon . . . you should know that. You were at the Blood Moon. Remember . . . it was a full moon that night."

She had a point. "So, is your pack all shifters or werewolves?"

"Werewolves."

"But your friends . . ."

"They are shifters, not of my pack, what are we to do?"

"I don't know. Go far away I guess. Where to . . . I don't know."

She held her hand out to me and I came to her side.

"Well, be ok. I promise."

I held her close. Hesitant at first, but gave in. She was small, frightened and very much a child who had lost her way.

I kissed her ear, then her neck. She moaned and relaxed more.

"Let me erase your fears tonight. Tonight you'll be mine."

She laid back. Eyes glistened. She was ready.

I leaned down and made light, tongue trails down her neck to where her pulse beat against her skin. The impulse to drink from her grew more and more intense. I knew that if I did, would send me off into an erotic frenzy from which I wasn't sure I could back off of.

"Jonathan . . . please . . . now." Came the breathy request.

"You sure?"

"Yes."

She opened the expanse of her gown and tilted her head to the side. Her skin, warm and soft and she smelled like Lilies of the Valley.

My hands, cold, touched her skin and she let out a gasp. Fingers traced the contours of her breast as I leaned in closer and closer. Her pulse beat against my tongue as I sucked gently on it.

I wanted to take her, body and soul right then and there. Make her mind forever.

My shirt, already opened by her hands that masterfully ripped it opened and whose legs now wrapped themselves around my waist. Damn, this girl wanted it bad.

"Not now. We must take our time."

"I don't want time. I need you now."

That's when I bit down.

Her body shook as I begun to drink. She tasted of fine wine with metallic notes, but sweet and I found it to be irresistible. The more I drank the more excited I became. Muscle grew taut and my vampiric mode set in, at a rate faster than I had anticipated.

This, drinking of human blood can be and is extremely erotic. You may not think so, but every muscle, every bodily function that gets excited sexually, is ten times that. The one who is being bitten can have the same experience, but it's usually aided with intercourse, which happened immediately.

I had stopped myself from taking too much from her. Her condition, though better, was not where it should have been when this happened, but we both needed it.

When finished, we lay there, curled in each other's arms and sated thoroughly. I was ready to go again, but I – I held back. Mustn't get too greedy.

"You alright?" I asked.

She looked up at me. "Very. In fact, I could go another round." Her fingers started trailing to places that awakened quickly.

I took hold of her hands immediately.

"Look, you're just getting over from being quite sliced up, literally, in fact, you almost died. I think it best to take things slow. You need to conserve your energy."

"My energy is just fine. You don't understand wolves. We like intimacy. The more, the better. You, my friend, are . . . let's just say, that you have the body that women dream of. I want to take advantage of that."

"Well, I'm not going anywhere, so you'll have plenty of time to play with me. In the meantime . . . rest."

She pouted as I got up to get my robe.

I looked down at her. Her body, though scarred, was still beautiful to behold. "I'm going to take a shower."

19

*M*ore trouble started soon after Vanessa was well enough to go out again.

She wanted to go back to live at her own place. I disagreed, seeing how it was one of her own that attacked her and without me being by her, it could happen again . . . only this time they would kill her.

I found that she had an apartment close to where I lived, which made me feel somewhat better, but I still had my doubts.

She lived downtown, above a restaurant. A popular place, from what I could see. It was an Italian restaurant, complete with grapes hanging from its ceiling and empty wine bottles used as candle holders on the tables.

As we went up the flight of stairs that led to her door at the top, you could smell the garlic and pasta which wafted up after us.

"How can you stand living here? I mean, smelling this every day and night would drive me insane."

"I love Italian food, so I don't mind. Come on . . ."

She opened the door.

"Let me go in first. You never know if someone is there inside."

Reluctantly, she motioned with her arm for me to take the lead. Upon entering, I noticed that she wasn't a very good housekeeper. Clothes, shoes and an array of other things scattered about, made it look like a hurricane had come through.

"You're not very tidy are you?" As I carefully stepped over her stuff.

"What are you talking . . . about . . . I didn't leave my apartment like this. I am the neatest, neat freak on earth. Someone had been here."

"Charlotte I bet."

"How do you know Charlotte?" She asked.

"While you were recovering, I went to the college and scoped out your friends. They're not very bright. They mentioned her in a conversation. It would seem she didn't, as well as the others, liked how you went against your pack rules. She's the one who ripped into you and brought you to my house. I'm guessing she found out about us."

Her face . . . motionless. Too flabbergasted I guess.

"Now can you see why I don't want you here? You can't stay, you have to come with me."

"I-I can't. They . . . she . . ."

She ran into, what I assumed, was her bedroom. Drawers were being opened and shut in a hurried fashion. She was looking for something.

I stood in the doorway, watched in alarm. The panic on her face worried me.

"What's wrong? What are you looking for?" I asked.

"No, no, nononononono...they . . . I mean . . . *she* took it. I got to get it back.

"Took what?"

"My tiger's eye stone. The one my mother left me. It's gone. I've always kept it on my night stand, in a box."

Confused as to the importance of this stone. Sentimental value came to mind, but her reaction to it being gone . . . seemed a bit much, but then again what do I know.

"We'll get it back once I have dealt with her."

She rushed out of the room. I, in tow. The loss of her mother's stone took such a toll on her. I couldn't get her to sit or calm down.

"You don't understand. The stone is my talisman. I-I didn't have it with me the night I was attacked and I should have. Now, look at me."

"You're right. I don't understand."

I went over to hold her but proved to be a bad move. Her eyes darkened to an inky black . . . vampiric in likeness, while a throaty growl came forth. Her stance, low, arms outstretched on either side and her knees bent, in a crouch position. Fighting mode.

"Whoa . . . easy now, I'm just the peace keeper. I want to help remember?"

She seemed to relax . . . a little, but I kept my distance. Pissing off a woman is one thing. Pissing off someone of her kind is just asking to die.

"It protects me. It was hers, my mother. She gave it to me the night before she died."

All at once she fell to her knees and wept. I rushed over to comfort when she stopped me.

"Stop, just . . . stop. It was all my fault she died. Had she not given me her stone, she'd still be here. Now, I have no one."

I wanted to say she had me but didn't.

"Um, what made you forget to wear it?"

The look in her eyes said so much.

"You . . . us. I didn't know what to do. The connection. It

had been bothering me since that night at the Blood Moon. I hadn't been myself, even my friends noticed the change. They kept asking questions and I lied. Told them I needed sleep," then she smiled, ". . . too much sex."

"Then, all the more reason for you not to stay here. Gather your things and let's get out of here."

She didn't pack much, just the necessities and stood in the middle of the living room for one more last look.

"It's not like you're never coming back." I tried to reassure her as I wrapped my arm around her.

"I know. Last time I felt this alone was when my mother had been killed."

This time I said it. "You're not really alone, you have me remember? I won't let anything happen to you. Promise."

This seemed to bring some comfort to her.

"Let's go."

With the door safely locked behind us. It wasn't just her being alone, it was *us*. She had her pack that ousted her from them and I, deceiving my own for finding a soulmate that wasn't pure . . . she was a hybrid. Something Domencio would not allow.

---

20

*T*he days went by slowly. Neither one of us dared to stay out for any length of time. I still needed to hunt, but I got by with animal blood, not that it sustained me, but at least I wouldn't die. Vanessa, she didn't need the blood like me. She does crave it like a person would crave their favorite food, but she prepared simple meals. All of which smelled delicious, but I don't like I use to. If I do have a meal, it's mostly vegetables, a lite broth, and raw meat, like smoked salmon. A nice glass of red wine is always a must. I've gotten to be quite the connoisseur. My favorite wine is Inglenook Cabernet Sauvignon 1941. At $24,675 it better be! I have a few in my cellar.

I had been in my study, reading the newspaper. Something I hadn't done in a long time when Vanessa came in.

"We need groceries."

Not looking up, I continued to immerse myself in the news but did answer her.

"Ok . . ."

"So, I won't be gone long."

"Ok . . ."

"You don't mind?"

Here I am, trying to read about the fires in California and I'm getting bombarded with questions that really don't need to be asked.

"Vanessa, if you think we need food, then get some. What's with all the questions?"

"Aren't you concerned about my pack or your friends attacking?"

She had a point, but the times we'd been out things had been ok, so I felt safe that nothing would happen. Besides, Vanessa had been healed for several weeks, her strength was back and I felt pretty secure in her abilities.

I set my paper down. Looked up at her and responded, "Go. You'll be alright. I feel it and besides the store is just a few blocks away. I can't imagine anything happening. Just hurry back."

With that, she leaned down, kissed me and left.

Two hours had gone by and she hadn't come back. I despised myself for letting her go. Why did I let her? Why? I had to go look for her. I knew she wasn't hurt, simply because of our connection I would have felt something and I didn't, so that part I felt happy about. Still didn't like the length of time it took to buy groceries.

Now, I know women and stores. Doesn't matter what kind of store it is, they take their time and look at *everything*.

Even if they don't need it, they look. I don't get it. When I go, I have what I want in my head. I go to the store, buy it, then it's back home . . . not that I shop a lot, but there have been a couple times.

"I'm home! Sorry, I took so long, but they had . . ."

All the worry I had geared up, vanished at the sound of her voice.

"What took you so long? I thought something bad happened. In fact, I was ready to go out . . . wait . . ." Something felt wrong. I didn't feel our connection. I couldn't read her thoughts.In truth, I couldn't *feel* her. This was a shifter. A shifter to look like Vanessa, which means, Vanessa had been taken, which was my worst fear. Now, she stood before me, though I don't think she realized that I know she's a fake. Ok, two can play this game.

"Wait for what? Did you miss me? Let me make it up to you? I'll make you forget everything." Her voice, subtle, but not quite like Vanessa's.

"I'm sure you could. You're hot. How come?"

"I guess you just turn my juices on. What do you say?"

This bitch was going to see what a mistake this was. First, get a little action. I mean, why denied fresh blood, when it comes so willingly.

I treated her like I would any other prey. I caught her attention with my eyes and my stunning good looks. Vampires are known for their fine, chiseled features and eyes that drink their prey in for the kill. Why even our voices cannot be ignored. It's music. It's our hook. We're the hottest species out there.

Once I had her in my clutches, I pulled her in . . . close. I leaned in. My cold breath left goosebumps upon her skin, as my tongue, delicately trailed the length of her neck. I stopped, just at the place where the carotid artery pulsed against the skin. It's rhythm . . . beat . . . by . . . beat started to excite the vampire in me. The frenzy.

She clung to me. Pressing me into her. Wanting more and more. Till she pressed me too far and I became more fierce, more powerful than I had ever been. She brought out the best and the worst in me and for that, she would get them both.

In whispered tones, I spoke my desire for her. Told her how delicious she tasted, how the sound of her heart made me wild with passion. This she believed.

"Now, my flower. The nectar that is you, your skin, soft, delicately scented, burns deep. I want you. I want you like I have never wanted any other woman."

"Oh, please. Talk no more, but show me instead. Enough talk."

"Get ready . . ."

She closed her eyes in anticipation. I had her right where I wanted. Vulnerable, hot and blinded by the throws of passion. Then, without hesitation, I ripped the front of her dress wide open. Her skin glistened.

Unbeknownst to her, while her eyes closed, anticipating the moment of passion that my loins would offer, got a rude awakening.

Down I went, as my fangs bit her left breast. Blood and muscle, splattered my face as I tore opened her chest. Her eyes flew opened. A blood-curdling scream filled the room as I looked down at this bitch. I scored.

"W-what are you doing? Y-you can't kill me I'm . . ."

"You're who bitch? Vanessa? Think again."

Down I went for a second bite. This time it was her right breast. Succulent as they were, her blood soured in my mouth. I spat it out.

"Before I finish you off, you *will* tell me where she is or if not, I will make you suffer. Bite by bite, till there is not a scrap of muscle left on you."

The fear in her eyes told me she would tell me anything, but whether it is true or not I could not say. I think I better sample some more for good measure.

Her screams were relentless. Her blood soaked my floor as I sucked every putrid mouthful.

"Stop! Please! Stop, I'll tell. I'll tell!" Her sobs deterred me not. I would have kept on drinking no matter what, but I had to. Had to know what they did to Vanessa. My soulmate.

I stopped. Long enough to listen.

"Tell me then. Is she with your pack? I know where it is."

Her sobs continued. She didn't have long. Between me drinking and the spillage continuing to flow, she infuriated me.

"TELL ME!"

"S-she's with . . . Domencio."

My hand flew to her throat in a vice like grip. Air, wheezed from her, as she tried to speak in breathy gasps.

"He . . . he . . . threatened my . . . my pack," she sucked in for more air that was not forth coming, "Said . . . he would k-kill us all . . . if we didn't . . . tell u-us who had killed his family."

"So, just like that, you gave her to him? Your own?"

"S-she betrayed us. B-betrayed us for . . . YOU."

"You whore!"

Then I bit down. Hard. On my favorite spot . . . the neck. Her body jerked and twisted as I did more than drank her blood. I ripped her to shreds. There was nothing left that would be recognized as a human. Then, took what little was left of her outside and burned her. I wretched up her foul blood when all was done.

I headed directly to Domencio. Somehow I had to get Vanessa out. Alive. Me as well. This would prove tricky as I am not well liked there anymore and I'm sure Luther has told

Domencio all about Vanessa and I. This wasn't going to be easy.

The house from the outside looked empty, as always, but this time something strange stirred within me as I approached it. Something deadly. No, not Vanessa, I still felt that connection. I didn't welcome this feeling at all.

I let myself in. All was still, dark, no movement anyway. It would seem as if the place were void of all vampires, but I knew better. They were all here.

Down into the crypt, I crept. Slow, quiet, ready for any attack that may come about. There were none, not until I opened the doors to Domencio's vault did I see him. He sat in his chair, arms rested on either side of him and his wings, outstretched behind him. Spears gleamed at the tips of each one. Ready for any false move on my part. I did not see Vanessa.

"My prodigal son has returned I see. Come to beg forgiveness from his father?"

He hadn't used that term of endearment, son, for years. Now, I wonder why? It would seem that he enjoyed being sarcastic tonight. That I could deal with. The blows I might receive from him, not so much.

Like him, I thought I'd address him as Father, something I hadn't done in years. He wasn't my biological father per-say, but he did treat me lovingly *like* any father would.

"Father . . ."

"DO NOT CALL ME BY THAT NAME! You are no son of mine. You have betrayed me and my house and for that, I cannot and will not forgive you."

A crowd soon gathered. I, in the centered of them all. Directly over the grate where sacrifices are made. I feared this to be my last day.

"Bring in the woman," Domencio said.

Within minutes, shuffling and the sound of chains grew

louder and louder, till there she stood. Beaten, scarred and chained like a dog. They threw her to the ground.

"This is who you call . . . your *soulmate*? Well, is it?"

"Yes, but she's a hybrid. She's part vampire and a shapeshifter."

Domencio stood up. Heavy swoosh noises pulsated from his bat like wings. They extended 8 feet on either side of him and grew larger as they shot forward and pierced Vanessa's shoulders and brought her toward me.

Her screams echoed. High, shrills that pained my ears. When Domencio released her, she fell at my feet. A wounded shell of her former self. She looked weak. Helpless.

"Vanessa, I'm so sorry. So, so, sorry."

Anger, along with sorrow, pinched the back of my throat as I spoke. All the while, thoughts of how we could resolve this ran through my mind.

"Grab Jonathan and chain him to the wall. He will watch his *soulmate* die before his very eyes."

"No, wait! Please, Father, I beg you. She's done no harm!"

"SHE HAS KILLED MEMBERS OF THIS HOUSE! Do not claim her innocence."

I didn't let them take me. I changed into my pure self, the vampire my Father helped create and I fought them all. I'd prove to him that I am his son. I am Jonathan, son of Domencio.

Three came at me. Gorging on my last victim before I came, my body grew bulkier than normal vampires. Eyes, bright red and keener, as well as my stealth. They couldn't keep up with me. It wasn't until the end that I and Luther were left to finish out the battle.

"I don't want to fight you. You're my brother." I didn't. We've been through too much to end it in someone's death.

His brow, furrowed with anger, pain, and regret, spoke, "You betrayed all of us. You betrayed me most of all. How could you? She's . . . *nothing*. She's only good for one thing . . ."

"Don't say it, or you'll regret it."

". . . fuck."

That was it. Crouched down in fight mode, we glared, hissed and launched ourselves at each other. I slammed him into the wall first. The web like crack extended outward where he hit, which landed him hard on the floor.

Blood was the lubrication of life, but also death, and I gloried in it. I no longer viewed Luther as my brother. He was my enemy.

He came at me. Not as fast as I expected, but the devastating blow sent me to the ground. He hit hard and strong, but I was stronger.

As he hurled himself at me. My quick reflexes kicked him straight in the stomach and he doubled over in pain. Enough time to finish him off.

My hatred gnawed my insides. It was as if the fires of hell stoked the hate in my heart. I looked at Luther, then I did the unthinkable. A tactic my Father taught me. In one swift movement, Luther's face had frozen in a terrified scream as it rolled away from his body.

The inner torment that I held deep within showed in my face just then. My heart ached with the loss of my friend and my voice was sick with sorrow.

"Satisfied . . . *Father*?" I couldn't look at him.

A sardonic laugh erupted from his throat, as he sat there. The whole fight seemed to give him pleasure. The old man, for he was hundreds of years old, gloomed and glowered at me from his chair. I wanted to slap his face off. Probably could if given the opportunity, but only a fool would try such a feat.

"You surprise me, but then you always did."

"I wish you no harm." There I said it. I truly didn't. I only wanted to leave with Vanessa and never return. He could continue his sordid life without me. Banish me if he will. I didn't care anymore.

"Bring her to me."

Three of his biggest army, as it were, dragged her over.

"Please, leave her be!"

"Enough! Chain her to the floor."

*F*all started. Leaves that had turned, fell to the ground like spilled paint. Death. That's what it reminded me of. That and the cold it brought, entombed the world with its bitterness. I hated it. As I hated my life.

I am, again, alone. Like I had been so long ago. Left to my own devices, in a place where I don't belong.

I'd been out to the forest preserve. Lunch.

Though it satisfied my hunger, it wasn't pleasurable.

Now, revenge was the only thing left and I reveled in its white-hot fury. I can't get it out of my head. Her tortured brain screamed with shrill cries, as I watched her die before me and my Father . . . stood with no remorse for my loss. The fires of hell will keep his company when I am through with him.

Home finally, and though it is not a welcomed one, I find some comfort in my room.

I lay on what was ours. A shared life that had become short lived. Her scent still clung to the blankets.

"DAMN YOU FATHER!"

The cancer of hate gnawed on my last nerve. I couldn't

take it anymore. Soon, I'd explode if I didn't silence his life, that took my soulmate.

No sooner did that thought came, that I found myself in front of my Fathers. I stood there, for the longest time, and all the while, the hate-bomb ticked inside me, waiting to go off.

"I will make them pay . . . in blood."

I was a man possessed. It was all a blur. Her death drove me.

Bodies became flame-blackened mummies within seconds. All around me, the ghastly inferno raged and my Father, a hellfire of living death raged over his body, charring him black. I had no regret. None.

I had to smile, maybe even laugh a little. The thought came to me as I stood there watching my father's house crumble to the ground, that the flames wrapped my enemy like presents at the devil's birthday party.

And a fir-wood that I know, from dawn to sunset-glow,
Shall whisper to a lonely sea, that swings far, far below.
Death, thy dawn makes all things new. Hills of Youth, I
    come to you,
Moving through the dew, moving through the dew.
Alfred Noyes

Dear reader,

We hope you enjoyed reading *Night Games*. Please take a moment to leave a review, even if it's a short one. Your opinion is important to us.

Discover more books by Sue Mydliak at https://www.nextchapter.pub/authors/sue-mydliak

Want to know when one of our books is free or discounted? Join the newsletter at http://eepurl.com/bqqB3H

Best regards,

Sue Mydliak and the Next Chapter Team

You might also like:

A New Time by Sue Mydliak
To read the first chapter for free, please head to:
https://www.nextchapter.pub/books/a-new-time

ABOUT THE AUTHOR

 Sue Mydliak lives in Illinois with her husband and has been writing for 14 years now. She started writing when the book Twilight first came out and fell in love with the paranormal genre. Since then, she has written and finished her Rosewood Trilogy and just recently her anniversary edition, Forever, which is the first book re-written for adults.

Currently, she has two books in progress, <u>Southern Shorts</u> which is an anthology of short stories about Dry Prong, Louisana and Night Games. Both will be out next year.